$17.89

⅔/08

YO-YO
MAN

BY DANIEL PINKWATER
ILLUSTRATED BY JACK E. DAVIS

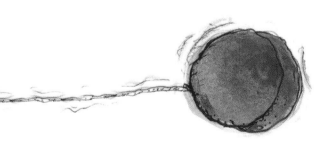

HARPERCOLLINSPUBLISHERS

Yo-yo Man • Text copyright © 2007 by Daniel Pinkwater • Illustrations copyright © 2007 Jack E. Davis • Manufactured in China. • All rights reserved. No part of this book may be used or reproduced in any manner whatsoever without written permission except in the case of brief quotations embodied in critical articles and reviews. For information address HarperCollins Children's Books, a division of HarperCollins Publishers, 1350 Avenue of the Americas, New York, NY 10019. • www.harpercollinschildrens.com • Library of Congress Cataloging-in-Publication Data • Pinkwater, Daniel Manus, 1941– Yo-yo man / by Daniel Pinkwater ; illustrated by Jack E. Davis.-- 1st ed.   p. cm. • Summary: Third grade improves dramatically for a boy after he makes up his mind to win the upcoming yo-yo tournament. • ISBN-10: 0-06-055502-5 — ISBN-10: 0-06-055503-3 (lib. bdg.) ISBN-13: 978-0-06-055502-3—ISBN-13: 978-0-06-055503-0 (lib. bdg.) [1. Yo-yos--Fiction. 2. Bullies--Fiction. 3. Schools--Fiction.] I. Davis, Jack E., ill. II. Title. PZ7.P6335Ynn 2007 [E]—dc22 2005017796 • CIP • AC • Design by Stephanie Bart-Horvath • 1 2 3 4 5 6 7 8 9 10 ❖ First Edition

It is the first day of school. The first day of third grade. I feel a sharp pain. Someone is twisting my arm. And I smell cinnamon candy. Oh no! It is cinnamon-Red-Hots-candy-sucking Richard Newton!

"Who is your master?" Richard Newton asks.

"Owww!" I say.

"Who?" he asks, puffing cinnamon in my ear.

"You are! You are!" I wail.

The bell rings. We go in. Oh no! Richard Newton sits right behind me. Third grade is going to be ugly. Mrs. Mousetrap starts right in with spelling words and math tests.

Finally it is time for recess.

Out on the playground a man has set up a sign:
RAMON: WORLD YO-YO CHAMPION.
Ramon swings two spinning yo-yos in wide circles,
makes them bounce and bob and roll along the ground.
The strings make a whispering, humming sound.

WORLD Y-Y CHAMPION

The morning sunlight makes the shiny yo-yo paint flash and sparkle. We kids feel ourselves getting lighter. We feel as though we are spinning, flying, sparkling too.

Ramon says, "Kids, use a King Tut Royal Egyptian Yo-yo, and you can do these tricks." Then Ramon uses four yo-yos. We go crazy.

Ramon hands out books. Free of charge! They tell how to do every trick, the easiest ones first, then the harder ones, then the hardest. Stamped on the back of each of Ramon's books is a blue stamp: King Tut Royal Egyptian Yo-yos AVAILABLE AT BILL'S TOYLAND.

Then Ramon tells us, when he comes back, any kid who can do every trick in the book will be given a gold yo-yo just like his, with realistic diamonds on each side.

And . . . a signed certificate, signed by Ramon himself!

After school kids crowd into Bill's Toyland.

I buy a smooth, shiny, heavy, perfect, beautiful, genuine deep red one.

The playground is a world of yo-yos. They are spinning and bobbing, whizzing and bouncing, sailing through the air. The strings hum and hiss. Every kid is learning the tricks from Ramon's book.

Richard Newton is helpless.
He is clumsy. He can't learn
a single trick. He is a yo-yo
no-go, a yo-yo goo-goo.

Richard's lack of yo-yo know-how makes him seem less scary.

I know exactly what I am going to do.

I am going to become a yo-yo genius. I am going to become a yo-yo go-go, with yo-yo know-how. I am going to learn all the tricks in the book. I am going to get the golden prize when Ramon comes back.

And for good measure, I am going to memorize more spelling words than anyone else, and make mincemeat of Mrs. Mousetrap.

MISSISS
IPI

Weeks go by. More weeks go by. Even though he does not know that I have learned every yo-yo trick—and he has learned two— Richard Newton has already stopped trying to bully me.

I am the best speller in the third grade, and Mrs. Mousetrap does not scare me much.

ELOQUENT
HALIBUT
DYNAMIC
CONDOR
HERO

And now . . . Ramon comes back. A true *yo-yo* man, he keeps his word, of course. There is a sign outside school: YO-YO TOURNEY TODAY!

We kids show the tricks we have learned, starting with the easy baby tricks. Each trick is harder, and when a kid makes a mistake, he or she is out of the tourney.

Do I have to say it? I am perfect. I am beautiful.
I do every trick, right to the end, right to the
double flip-flop flying bouncing sleeper.

There are tears in Ramon's eyes as he gives
me my golden yo-yo with diamonds.
Everyone admires me. I am a true yo-yo man.

And I can spell.